BISTRO

SPECIAL OF
THE DAY

FROG
LEGS

This story begins in a frightful way—
"Frog legs—special of the day."

Philippe

In Monet's Garden

by **Lisa Jobe Carmack**

illustrated by **Lisa Canney Chesaux**

Museum of Fine Arts, Boston

In the city of Paris, as everyone knows,
frog legs are eaten, except for the toes.
They are buttered and baked, and sometimes fried,
and the bigger the better is always the guide.

A train ride away in the French countryside,
lived a frog named Philippe with a marvelous stride.
He got his name because of his leap,
which was the biggest and grandest, just like his feet.

Philippe liked to play in his pond every day,
and he tried not to mind when his friends were unkind. . .

"Tee-hee, ha-ha,
you're a dumb looking frog,"
they teased the unhappy Philippe.
"Your thighs are too long,
your shape is all wrong.
You can't be our friend,
you just don't belong."

The frog catcher crept
with his big trusty net
as they bullied Philippe
and made fun of his feet.

"Oh no, it's not fair," they cried in despair. "Philippe in your net is a far better bet!"

"Big feet or not, I haven't been caught.
These legs won't be buttered and baked, or fried.
But as for you, well, I bid you good-bye."

"Leap, leap, Philippe,"
he heard the sheep bleat.
And he kept on hopping,
there was no time for stopping,
as he made his escape
from a gruesome fate.

Trois

Just when Philippe
was all out of leap,
he came to the gate
of the Monet estate.
And reading the sign,
which suited him fine,
he begged Monet's pardon
and entered the garden.

"Oh my, what a size!
I can't believe my eyes,"
exclaimed the painter Monet.
"What a physique!
Those legs are *très magnifique!*
You're the perfect addition...
to my garden...not my kitchen!"

Philippe's grin grew a mile wide.
He wouldn't be buttered and baked, or fried.
This smile became his only expression,
because Monet's garden made quite an impression.

Monet showed him the pond
of which he was fond,
where he painted the light
between daybreak and night.
And as for Philippe,
there were bugs of all kinds,
green ones and pink ones
on which he could dine.

So Philippe found a home to call his own,
and Monet added some green to his painterly scene.

Claude Monet was a famous painter who lived more than 100 years ago. He lived in France, in a country town. He loved bright colors, so he planted many different kinds of flowers in his garden. He dug a pond and filled it with water so that he could paint the sky and trees reflected there.

Monet planted beautiful water lilies in the pond. Their leaves floated on the water, and yellow, pink, and white flowers bloomed on top of the leaves.

Monet loved to paint with bright colors, too. He painted pictures of the water lilies in his pond by dabbing bits of color side by side. When you stand back, you can see the shape of a flower, but when you look close, you see strokes of paint. Look at how Monet used blue and purple and pink and yellow and green!

These pages: *Water Lilies (Nymphéas),* 1907, Oil on canvas; 89.3 x 93.4 cm (35 1/8 x 36 3/4 in.), Bequest of Alexander Cochrane. 19.170

©1998 Museum of Fine Arts, Boston

Art Direction by Lisa Jobe Carmack

10 9 8 7 6

First published in 1998 by the Museum of Fine Arts, Boston
Department of Retail Publications
295 Huntington Avenue
Boston, Massachusetts 02115

ISBN 0-87846-456-5

Printed and bound in Hong Kong